# The FOOTBALL GHOSTS

Malachy Doyle

Garry

# Dedication
# For Ben and Polly
# M.D.
# For Moyna
# G.P.

www.malachydoyle.co.uk

## EGMONT
*We bring stories to life*

**Book Band: White**

First published in Great Britain as 'Famous Seamus and the Football Ghosts' in
Magical Tales of Ireland by Hutchinson 2003
This edition published 2007 by Egmont UK Ltd
239 Kensington High Street, London W8 6SA
Text copyright © Malachy Doyle 2007
Illustrations copyright © Garry Parsons 2007
The author and illustrator have asserted their moral rights
ISBN 978 1 4052 2749 0
10 9 8 7 6
A CIP catalogue record for this title is available from the British Library.
Printed in Singapore.
44596/6

# Contents

Red Bananas

# A Tent Full of Sheep

That's me in the picture - famous Seamus!

I suppose you're thinking I'm a bit young to be famous, but wait till you hear my story.

And that old fellow next to me, the one with the beard, that's my Granda. Not half as brave as me, but he's always ready and willing to join me in my favourite pastime – going for long long walks in the middle of the night.

Well, one Saturday me and my Granda were up in the hills, camping. It was a cold and blowy night but there we were, all cosy warm in our sleeping bags, when a dark shape appeared in the doorway.

'Who's that?' said my scaredy-ba Granda. 'Who's that at the door, Seamus?'

Jeepers!

'Ah, it's nothing but a poor old sheep,
coming in out of the wind,' said I.

Then in walked
another sheep.

Followed by
another, and
another.

'Let's go for one of your night-time walks, Seamus,' said my Granda, scrambling to his feet. 'For we won't be getting any sleep here tonight.'

So up we got and out we went, past a great line of shivering woollies, all queuing up to get in from the cold.

I led my Granda through the pitch-dark night, over the river and all the way to a farmhouse.

'Is there anyone in?' I cried, banging on the door.

Hello?

There was a long long silence, but it creaked open at last and a craggy face appeared. It was an old fellow, older than my Granda even, and he was dressed in his pyjamas.

# Elvis and a Dead Pig

The farmer put another log on the fire, and I asked him my favourite question.

'So what two things do you like most in the world?' I said.

'Well . . .' He scratched his chin. 'There's Tommy Riley up there . . .' and he pointed to a fading photo of a pig above the fireplace.

'Dead and gone now, but my pride and joy for many a long year. Best friend I ever had.'
'Your best friend was a pig?' I said, amazed.
'Indeed he was, lad.'

'And what's the second, then? What's your second best thing?'

'Oh, that'd be Elvis Presley,' said the farmer.

'Who's Elvis Presley?' I asked him. 'Another pig?'

'Another pig!' cried my Granda, with a mighty snort.

'Sure wasn't he the King of Rock and Roll, boy? Wasn't he the greatest singer that ever lived?'

And he jumped up from his chair, grabbing the old farmer's guitar.

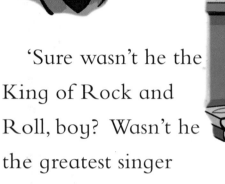

'So what about you, young Seamus?' said the farmer, still laughing. 'What's your two favourite things, then?'

'Ghosts and United,' I told him, quick as a flash.

'Ghosts and United . . .' he said slowly. 'Well, there's a strange thing!'

'Sure it's not half as strange as Elvis Presley and a dead pig!' I told him.

I love United!

'All I mean is,' said he, 'that it's a strange
thing you turning up here tonight, if it's
ghosts and United you're after.'

'Why's that?' asked my Granda.

'Well . . .' said the farmer, 'did you see that
big castle up on the hill?'

'Too dark,' said my Granda.

'Did you hear anything, then?'

'Too windy.'

'Well that's where you ought to be, young man, if it's ghosts and soccer you're after.'

'How do you mean?' said I.

'I mean . . .' said the old farmer, 'that that old castle's full of ghosts.  Ghosts playing football.'

'Footballing ghosts!' I cried, amazed.

'It's the truth,' said he. 'As sure as I'm standing here before you in my jammies.'

# The Ghosts of United

My Granda got up and put another log on the fire. 'So what about United, then?' he asked the old farmer. 'Where do they come into the story?'

'Sure that's who they are!' said the man. 'The ghosts of the 1948 team.'

'What?' said my Granda, turning pale. 'The year Stanley Ramsbottom was captain? The year they lost the Cup Final to the Rovers? Sure it nearly broke my heart. It can't be them – you're only pulling my leg.'

'I wish I was,' said the farmer. 'Because every Saturday night for the last I-don't-know-how-many years there's never a wink of sleep to be had in this here house for all the terrible noise coming from up on that there hill.

What a racket!

'Kicking a football, they are, them downstairs and the Rovers up. Echoes, it does, all the way down the hill, all the way up the stairs, and all the way into my poor tired ears.'

'Shush then,' I whispered, 'and let's have a listen.'

But all we could hear was the howling of the wind.

I can't hear them.

'Come on, Granda ...' I said, when the farmer went out to top up the teapot.

We'd better go and see.

'We'll just go up to the castle and have a quick look. Sure there's probably nothing there.'

He's not too fond of ghosts, my scaredy-ba Granda, but I knew he'd have to come with me, for he'd promised Mum he wouldn't let me wander off on my own.

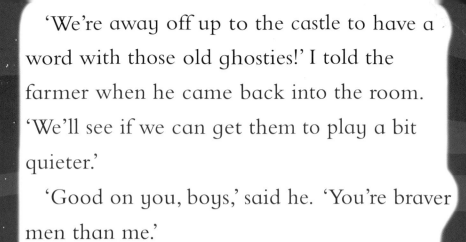

'We're away off up to the castle to have a word with those old ghosties!' I told the farmer when he came back into the room. 'We'll see if we can get them to play a bit quieter.'

'Good on you, boys,' said he. 'You're braver men than me.'

So up we got and off we went. Trudging through the pitch-dark night, with my Granda holding on to me for dear life.

Good luck, boys!

'Listen . . .' I said. But there was nothing to be heard but the howling of the wind.

Then, 'Listen . . .' I said, as we got a bit nearer, but there was nothing to be heard but the baaing of a hundred sheep in a tent.

Baa!

Baa!

Then, 'Listen!' I said, and there it was. The thumping and banging, banging and yelling of ghosts. Ghosts playing football!

'I'm away back down for another cup of tea with the old farmer,' said my scaredy-ba Granda.

'Oh no you don't!' said I, grabbing his arm. 'You'll be safe enough with me.'

# Into the Haunted Castle

So in we went, through the big creaky door that looked like it hadn't been opened in a hundred years, down the cobwebby corridor and into the Great Hall of Narrow Water Castle.

And there before our eyes was the strangest sight you've ever seen. Eleven red and white ghosts, pushing a battered old football round the room, and each and every one of them dressed in the full 1948 kit, baggy shorts and all.

'Stanley!' yelled my Granda, and he ran over to the one with the captain's armband on, grabbed him by the hand and started pumping it up and down.

I can't believe it!

'Stanley Ramsbottom, my lifelong hero! Sure everyone thought you'd died years ago!'

'I did,' said the ghost grumpily. 'But they won't let me rest in peace. I have to go on and on kicking this stupid ball around till someone restarts the game.'

Could you sign this please?

I'd never heard of Stanley Ramsbottom, to tell you the truth, but if he played for United he's got to be good, so I reached deep down into the pocket of my coat and pulled out my autograph book. I always carry it with me on my night-time rambles – you never know who you might meet.

'There you go, lad,' said Stanley, signing his name. 'It's years since anyone asked me to do that.

Now if you two want to make yourselves useful, join in. We're exhausted!'

Please join us!

Stanley kicked the ball to my Granda, my Granda passed it to me, and I dribbled it all the way down the hall, past Albert Waddle, round Tony Barclay, and slammed it past the goalie, Safehands O'Sullivan.

'Not bad, Seamus,' said Stanley, coming up to me. 'We could have done with you in the final.'

'You're right, Stanley,' said my Granda. 'Wasn't I there with my very own Grandad, cheering you on. One nil to the Rovers! Sure I never got over it. I can still hear the sound of the final whistle, ringing in my ears.'

'But you can't!' cried Stanley. 'That's the whole point – the ref never blew the final whistle!

He had it in his mouth, and he was just about to check his watch when big Buster McBurney of the Rovers collided into him.

Erk!

The ref swallowed the whistle, someone in the crowd blew one of theirs, and everyone thought it was all over.'

'So you mean to tell me . . .' Granda could hardly believe his ears. 'That the match isn't finished yet? There's still a chance to win the Cup?'

'Exactly!' cried Stanley. 'And that's why we're here in this freezing old castle, kicking a ball around, us downstairs and the Rovers up, till some sort of a referee comes along and brings us all together to finish the match. Listen . . .'

And there, above our heads, was the sound of eleven ancient Rovers, pushing a tired old football around the room.

'Have no fear, Seamus is here!' I cried.

And I reached deep down into the pocket of my coat. For guess what else I always carry with me when I go on my night-time rambles? A whistle, in case I get lost!

'WHEEEE!'

Look!

# Famous Seamus, Superstar!

There was a terrific clatter of boots on the staircase, and in rushed another eleven baggy footballers.

'It's the Rovers!' cried my Granda, grabbing the whistle from my lips. 'Game on!' he yelled. 'It's one nil to the Rovers and there's only two minutes left.'

The twenty-two ghosts ran around like mad things, chasing the ball up and down the Great Hall, until 'Aaargh!'

Ow!

Albert Waddle fell in a heap on the floor, rubbing his leg. 'It's cramp,' he moaned. 'You'll have to take me off, captain.'

'But I can't,' said Stanley, looking desperately round the room. 'We haven't any substitutes.'

And then his ghostly
eyes fell upon me.
'Seamus . . .' he said, in a
voice full of promise.
'You're on, boy!'

'Me?'

So Albert tore off his shirt,
I threw it on, and there I was, playing centre
forward for United in the dying moments of
the 1948 final! A goal down and less than
two minutes to play!

'WHEEEE!' went my Granda and the ball came flying towards me. I chested it down, dummied the Rovers's left back and slammed it past the keeper. One all!

'WHEEEE!' went my Granda again, and the Rovers's centre forward kicked off from the spot, passing it to Buster McBurney, who came flying towards me.

Help, I thought, he'll flatten me. I'll be the one who'll have to rest in peace.

So I was all set to dodge out of his way at the last moment, when that old streak of bravery that always gets me in so much trouble took over. I stuck out my leg and tried to roll the ball off his foot, and it worked.

'Run, Stanley!' I yelled, floating the ball over to my captain and racing on towards goal, with big bad Buster puffing away behind me like a steam train. Stanley did a beautiful first-time overhead pass, straight to my head, and I whacked it with all my might into the top right-hand corner.

'WHEEE!' went my Granda, and the game was over. 2–1 to United!

'We've done it at last! We've won the Cup!' cried Stanley, hoisting me onto his shoulders.

Hip hip hooray!

'Three cheers for Famous Seamus!' he roared, taking me on a lap of honour round the room.

Everyone cheered, including the Rovers, who were just glad to finish the game at last. Even my Granda joined in, though he had to do it quietly, of course, because he was the referee.

You were great, Seamus!

And one by one, as the ghostly footballers came up to shake my hand, they disappeared into thin air, never to be seen again. So that all there was left in the Great Hall of Narrow Water Castle was me, my Granda, and the very football I'm holding in my hands before you.

Now do you see why I'm famous?